BABAR'S

LAURENT DE BRUNHOFF

ABC

To Rosemary Courtney,

Laurent Brunhoff

RANDOM HOUSE

Aa
airport

Alexander aims his **arrow at** the **apple**.

Arthur plays **an accordion**.

Bb
Babar

The **bear** reads a **book** in **bed**.

The **bird blows** out the candles on the **birthday** cake.

Cc
circus

The **cat climbs** onto the **camel**.

Celeste wears her **crown** when she drives her **car**.

The **crocodile cannot catch** the **crow**.

D d
dog

Sometimes a **doll** needs a **doctor**.

The **duck** beats the **drum**.

Ee
elephant

White rabbits have long pink **ears** and little pink **eyes**.

Ff
fire fighter

The **fox follows** the **footprints**.

The **frog** plays a **flute** in the **flower** garden.

Flora feeds the **fish**.

G g
giraffe

The **geese go** out the **garden gate**.

Hh
Halloween

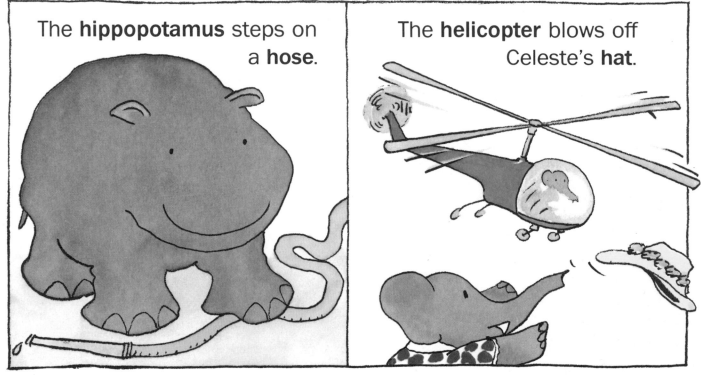

The **hippopotamus** steps on a **hose**.

The **helicopter** blows off Celeste's **hat**.

Ii

ice skating

Don't touch the hot **iron**!

Oops! Arthur spills the **ink**.

Jj
jungle

Zephir gets **jam** on his **jacket** when he **juggles** the **jars**.

Kk

kitchen

The **kangaroo** **kicks** the ball to the **koala**.

A **kitten** loves **kisses**.

Ll
ladder

The **little lamb licks** Pom's **lollipop**.

The **lazy lion lies** on the **log**.

Mm
merry-go-round

The **magician** **makes** the **monkey** change into a **mouse**.

Nn

nest

Hammering **nails** is **noisy!**

Cornelius **needs** a **net** to catch butterflies.

Oo

orchestra

This **ostrich** likes to eat **oranges**.

The **owl** and the **opossum** . . . sleep in the **oak** tree.

Babar has **oil** spots **on** his **overalls**.

Pp
playground

The **parrot perches** on the **palm** tree.

Pom paints a **picture** of a **peach**.

The **pretty peacock** is lost among the **penguins**.

This **pig** wears **purple**-striped **pajamas**.

Qq
queen

A **quilt** keeps the **queen** warm.

Rr
rhinoceros

Rabbits really like **radishes.**

This **reindeer** has a **red** nose.

S s
seashore

Squirrels do not like the **smell** of **skunks**.

Seals and **sharks** **swim** in the **sea**.

Tt
tugboat

The **tiger tells** stories on television.

The **turtle** rides **the tricycle**.

U u

unicorn

Alexander and Babar keep dry **under** their **umbrellas**.

Vv
van

Ww
wagon

X x
x-ray

Y y
yak

Zz
zebra

Zephir zips up his sleeping bag **zipper**.